All About Me

This Is My Family

By Meg Gaertner

www.littlebluehousebooks.com

Copyright © 2020 by Little Blue House, Mendota Heights, MN 55120. All rights reserved. No part of this book may be reproduced or utilized in any form or by any means without written permission from the publisher.

Little Blue House is distributed by North Star Editions:
sales@northstareditions.com | 888-417-0195

Produced for Little Blue House by Red Line Editorial.

Photographs ©: AzmanL/iStockphoto, cover; Mila Supinskaya Glashchenko/Shutterstock Images, 4, 16 (bottom right); wathanyu/iStockphoto, 7; romrodinka/iStockphoto, 8–9, 16 (top left); karelnoppe/Shutterstock Images, 11; ozgurdonmaz/iStockphoto, 12–13, 16 (bottom left); tdub303/iStockphoto, 15, 16 (top right)

Library of Congress Control Number: 2019908646

ISBN
978-1-64619-006-5 (hardcover)
978-1-64619-045-4 (paperback)
978-1-64619-084-3 (ebook pdf)
978-1-64619-123-9 (hosted ebook)

Printed in the United States of America
Mankato, MN
012020

About the Author

Meg Gaertner enjoys reading, writing, dancing, and being outside. She lives in Minnesota.

Table of Contents

This Is My Family 5

Glossary 16

Index 16

This Is My Family

This is my mom.

We like to play music.

This is my dad.

We like to dance.

This is my brother.

We like to ride bikes.

This is my sister.

We like to swing.

This is my grandma.

We like to read.

This is my grandpa.

We like to cook.

Glossary

brother

grandpa

grandma

mom

Index

B
brother, 8

D
dad, 6

M
mom, 5

S
sister, 10